STUCK IN
THE DARK

I0541033

a novel by

GWEN CANNON

G Publishing LLC
Detroit, Michigan

This novel is a work of fiction. Names, characters, places and incidents are the product of the author's imagination or are used fictitiously. Any resemblance to actual persons, living or dead, events, or locales, is entirely coincidental.

Edited by: Anthony Ambrogio

Cover Design: Brittany Janay Jackson

Published by G Publishing, LLC
P. O. Box 24374
Detroit, MI 48224

ISBN 13: 978-0-9820002-0-5
ISBN 10: 0-9820002-0-0

Library of Congress Control Number: 2008932731

Printed in the United States of America

www.gwencannon.net

ACKNOWLEDGMENTS

I would like to thank my creator, for giving me the guidance, vision, and strength to complete my second book. Thanks to my husband, James—baby you have been soooo supportive of me as I embark into the world of storytelling. You were out there in the streets hustling my first book, on the job and at the gym. Words cannot say how much I appreciate you. I know you got my back no matter what. Thanks to my mother, Mary Collins, who continues to be a blessing to me with her words of wisdom. I love you, Ma. Thanks to my niece, Catrea Carmichael, for pitching in with her artistic skills with the invitations and flyers for my book-release party. Thanks to my co-workers and friends Toyia Baker and Belinda Robinson for helping out with the bookmarks. Thanks to my family members for their support: my brother, Aaron Collins, and his wife, Lisa, in Atlanta; my niece Reese, my sisters, Rosemary, Roslin, Deborah. and Margie (and her husband, Kevin). Thanks to the Cannon family: Delana, Fay, Monique, Bryan, and his wife, Crystal. I would like to send out a big thank-you to my friend, my sister, Lettice Crawford and her husband James. We go 'way back. I knew I picked the right person to host my book-release party. I love you for being who you are—a strong, beautiful black woman. Thanks to my publisher, Julia Hunter, you are awesome. Thanks to everyone out there who supported me with my first book, *Everything That Looks Good Ain't Good for You.* You were there for me; even though some of you were not readers, you still showed your support, and I have much love for you.

INTRODUCTION

We meet people from all walks of life, from various cultural backgrounds. But do we really know who we are meeting? We sometimes even ask ourselves, "How much do I really know about this person?" It could be your co-worker, neighbor, or even a childhood friend. It could be your sister, brother, cousin, niece, or nephew.

What happens behind closed doors, after the lights go out, when you're sitting in the dark? I'm sure some of you have met someone at a club and got all hot and bothered because this brother/sister was looking tight. *Shittt*, they got it going on! Were you curious? —Hey, we all are! Don't sit there and act all high and mighty like your ass never wanted to test the waters. But is testing the waters worth it?

Now sit back and truthfully ask yourself that question. We all know curiosity gets the best of us, and it's certainly true that "Curiosity killed the cat." My mother used to tell me and my siblings that story all the time. Oh, my mother knew what she was talking about. I want you to come venture with me and my brothers and sisters along the road of being *Stuck in the Dark*, and then ask yourself if you were ever Stuck in the Dark about someone you thought you knew.

CHAPTER 1

"We'll be touching down at Detroit Metro Airport in about 15 minutes," the pilot announced over the intercom. I couldn't wait to get home and surprise my man. I decided to come home a day earlier, since I had finished ahead of schedule.

I knew, If I stayed in Vegas another day, I would have my ass at the roulette or black jack tables. One of my bad habits, since my younger days.

I blame it on my mother; she used to take the street numbers before we even had the state lottery. So she's the one who started me to gambling. I had everything in place to surprise Chris; I was going_to change into this sexy lingerie I had picked up in Vegas. I knew it ought to get his dick nice and hard, so he could take care of a sista well. Shit, right about now, I don't mind being knocked the fuck out with some good-ass sex.

"Please return to your seats, and fasten your seat belts for landing" said the flight attendant. About damn time! Shit, these flights from Vegas take long as hell. Shit—what is it—three or four hours?

Once we landed, I made a dash straight to the ladies room, changed into my fuck-me out-fit, and tied my coat closed. You know—how they do that shit in the movies. It looked sexy as hell.

I strutted through the airport with a big-ass smile on my face, just thinking about the hot sex I was about to get. I had been gone two weeks trying to tie up some last-minute business for the new company I was trying to launch by July.

"Damn! I'm having a helluva time trying to catch a cab! Of course this would happen when I'm horny as hell. Shit, I knew I should have driven my car and left it at the airport. But the parking fees are too damn high. Especially for two weeks. Where in the fuck are all the cabs? I can't believe there's not one fucking cab in front of the airport. Just my luck!"

Damn, was I talking out loud? Because this cutie over here is staring and smiling at me. "Um, excuse me—do you know me?" I asked.

"No, it's just that you were talking to yourself, I thought it was funny as hell," he said, smiling.

"Oh, I'm funny, huh? If you must know, I was fussing about not seeing a cab" I said.

"It looks like there's a cab coming this way now. I'll flag it down for you if you take my business card," he said.

"No thank you, I'm seeing someone."

"Oh, so, just because I ask you to take my card, you think I want to take you out. Look, sister, you're definitely cute and sexy, but don't put yourself out like that. I see now that a brother can't even try to market himself," he said.

"I'm sorry. I've been on a long flight, and I'm just trying to get home," I explained. *Not that it's any of his business. Shit, my pussy is throbbing for a long-ass hard dick. I can't wait to get home and jump Chris's ass.*

"Ok, now that we've cleared that up, can I give you my card? You never know when you might need legal consultation," he said.

"I just might need that; you never know," I said, smiling.

"Hmm, brother got it going on: Attorney James Patton. You don't look old enough to be an attorney," I said, still smiling, looking him up and down

"I get that response all the time. Trust me, I'm older than you think," he said as he whistled for the cab to stop.

"Yeah, right; you're probably younger than me," I said, taking his card.

"Hey, you never told me your name," he said as I was closing the cab door.

"Tina" I said as the cab driver watched me through the rear-view mirror.

"Where to, lady?" asked the taxi driver.

"23502 Parklane Drive," I said, settling back in the seat in my coat-covered lingerie.

Damn, that was the longest two weeks! I hope Chris is still up; I'm horny as hell. All I could think about was getting my groove on—you sistas know how it is when your shit be on fire and you need that strong hard dick to cool you off. My kitty was purring like hell—got to cool her ass off. Twirling the card around in my hand, I kept picturing Attorney Patton's smile. Brother definitely was a cutie. *Damn, this motherfucka is driving slow as hell.*

"Sir, can you go a little faster? I said

"I'm going as fast as I can, Ma'am" said the cab driver, frowning.

*   *   *   *   *

About damn time! I think his ass took the scenic route. Good, I see a light on upstairs. I hope Chris is still up. He must have had his boys over, I see someone left their Detroit Tigers baseball cap. I knew it didn't belong to Chris; he hated the Tigers. Damn, these squeaky-ass stairs are going to ruin my surprise. Oh hell, naw—is that moaning I hear coming from the bedroom? I know this motherfucka ain't got a hoe laid up in our bed!

As I approached the door, I could see this nigga doggy-styling on a bitch. Before I realized what I was doing, I ran over and snatched the covers off and started swelling on his ass.

"What the hell—" hollered Chris as he grabbed me.

"You up here fucking some bitch in our bed!" I screamed.

But it wasn't a bitch my man was fucking; he was butt-ass naked, pounding away up another nigga's ass.

CHAPTER 2

"Y'all nigga's ready to hoop?" asked Tim.

"Hell, yeah, you better bring your A-game with you, nigga!" said G.

"Is Chris coming?" hollered Rock

"I met up with him early yesterday, and he said he would be here. He said he was bringing his boy with him," said Tim.

"I hope his boy ain't no pussy and can hoop," said G.

"Well I'm ready to take a nigga's paycheck today," smiled Rock as he started doing laps around the gym.

"What up, nigga?" shouted Chris, coming into the gym

"About damn time! You know my wife be tripping already about me coming in late from our games. I told her the niggas be chilling, talking shit, and drinking brews after the game," said Tim.

"This my boy Mark I was telling you about," Chris introduced his friend.

"What up, dog?" G. greeted Mark.

"I'm ready to get my hoop on. Chris already gave me the scoop on y'all," said Mark

"Don't believe shit that nigga say," smiled Tim.

"Y'all niggas ready to get y'all ass whooped?" hollered Mike, as his team took the floor.

"Hey, dog, let's get this game started," enthused Tim.

And they sure as hell did.

* * * * *

"Wheewwwhhh, I'm tired as hell! I'm getting too old for this shit," wheezed Rock.

"Nigga, you ain't that old. I'm the oldest one out the crew, and your ass crying about playing one damn game!" Tim scolded him.

"Tracy probably wore your ass out last night!"

"Nigga, I can hang in that area," smiled Rock.

"Whatever, nigga," said G.

"The losing team gone buy a case of beer," said Tim.

"Yeah, yeah, yeah," smiled Mike.

"Mike, when is Jason getting out?" asked Rock.

"Next week. That nigga can't wait to come home. I'm still tripping how my brother got strung out at the casino and just fucking lost his mind. His ass had to do ninety days in jail for some stupid-ass shit."

"Yeah—what was that he did? Tried to snatch his money back from the dealer at the Black Jack table," laughed Rock.

"That shit was funny, but it wasn't funny when they showed that shit on TV. I thought they would never stop broadcasting that stupid shit. They probably was trying to use Jason as an example, showing his dumb ass telling the dealer to suck his dick and jumping across the table," said Mike.

"How Tina doing, Chris?" asked Tim.

"She all right," said Chris.

"When's the big date?" asked G.

"It was July 3rd, but her ass got mad at me last night."

"What your ass do now?" Rock asked Chris.

"Nothing! —Did Tracy say something to you about me and Tina?" asked Chris.

"*Naw*. Why?" asked Rock.

"Just curious. You know her and Tina always on the damn phone gossiping about something," said Chris, looking worried.

"Well, I don't know about y'all niggas, but wifey cooked dinner, and a nigga is hungry as hell," said Tim, heading for the exit.

"Damn, Tim, you know your ass lucked up! Women don't believe in cooking nowadays. Shit, Lisa got any sisters that cook? I can't get my friend to cook me shit; her ass always saying where we going to eat. I be feeling like saying, 'Maybe your ass need to learn how to fucking cook!'" said Mike, laughing

"Hey, I'll holler at y'all later; I gotta run," said Rock. "We can pick up that case another time."

Rock caught up with Tim.

"Chris' boy Mark, he look familiar; I know I seen him before," said Rock.

"Yeah, I was saying the same thing," Tim agreed. "Maybe we saw him at the bar or something."

"Mark was soft as hell on the court. Did you see how, every time somebody pushed him or bumped his ass, he was hollering 'Foul'?" asked Rock, laughing.

"Yeah, I peeked that, too," said Tim, imitating Mark.

"Chris can leave his ass at home next time," said Rock.

"Chris was telling me that Mark dance for a living," said Tim.

"What kind of dancing? I hope it ain't that ballerina shit," said Rock.

"Naw, a male stripper down at Striptease on Telegraph and 96," said Tim.

"What? —That's where Tracy be taking her ass sometimes. She probably know the nigga," said Rock.

"Shit, I don't know. Lisa went with Tracy and Tina a couple of times," said Tim.

"I don't know what they get out of that shit." Rock shook his head.

"Nigga, the same shit you get out of going to see them strippers every fucking Thursday at Shake That Ass," Tim told him.

"Man, I'll holla back," said Rock, laughing, as he got in his car.

"All right," said Tim.

CHAPTER 3

"Nigga, it's good seeing you. Damn, you got pumped up in just 90 days!" said Mike.

"Shit, wasn't nothing else to do but lift weights, read, watch TV, clean, and take my ass to bed," said Jason, flexing his muscles.

"You didn't let them niggas break your ass down in there, did you?" asked Mike

"Nigga, do I look like a pussy to you?"

"Naw, baby bro," Mike backed off. "I'm just saying I know what be happening to niggas when they on lock down for a minute."

"Shit, you know me, I'll go down fighting before I let a nigga break me in, you feel me? I can stroke my dick a few times if I really need to get off. Fuck that gay-ass shit. That ain't me, big bro. What's been going on since I left?"

"Nothing, same old shit. Niggas meeting up to hoop, going to the bar, and talking shit."

"You seen my girl Monica?"

"Shit, nigga, I wasn't out here baby-sitting for you and shit. I'm going to let you deal with Monica yourself and find out how she been doing," said Mike, looking suspicious

"What the fuck you mean, 'deal with Monica'?" hollered Jason

"Nigga, you better step off—I ain't the one you need to be hollering at. Don't think for a minute that because your ass gained some weight and a little muscle that I still can't take your ass down!"

"My bad, big bro, Jason apologized. "Did you see Monica with somebody?" he asked, concerned

"Naw, I just been hearing shit on the streets. That she be at that club Shake That Ass," said Mike

"What the hell she doing at that damn place? I know the fuck she ain't climbing a fucking pole, dancing for money. I left her ass more than enough money to get her by until I got out."

"Bro, just go on down to Shake That Ass tonight and see for yourself," said Mike

"You better go with me. I don't want to end back up in that fucking place over some stupid shit again. And don't let me drink shit tonight. I know, if I put some of that Patron in my system, I'm gone have that 'I-don't-give-a-fuck' attitude," said Jason

"I'll go with you, little bro," Mike said, pushing him out the door.

CHAPTER 4

I was in a state of shock. My baby, my man, my soon-to-be husband—fucking another nigga. The nigga he was fucking pulled the covers over his head. I guess he didn't want me to see who he was because he kept his head turned so that I couldn't see his face.

"Oh, hell, naw! I want to see what man— *not woman*—has taken my place between the sheets!" I screamed, tugging at the bedclothes Tears started to form in the corners of my eyes. I couldn't believe what I saw. Chris was fucking my ex—yes, you heard me right. My ex-man, Mark. I just stood there in a state of shock. I couldn't believe my fucking eyes.

"Tina, let me explain—"Chris began

"What the fuck is there to explain, Chris? You should have told me you were fucking gay, and, to top the shit off, I didn't know my ex preferred a hard-ass dick up his ass, or I could have strapped on a dildo and made him happy!"

"Tina, I'm sorry—" said Mark

"Mark, I kind of felt you had feminine ways, but I blew that shit off. I thought you were just overly neat and shit for a man. You would talk about how buff and tight a nigga's body was. That shit definitely made me wonder. I used to ask, 'Why the fuck is my man making comments about another nigga's body?' That's something me and my home-girl would do, but I guess my assumptions were right. I knew you danced for a living, but I would have never though you fucked men!"

"You're right, Tina; I should have said something."

"I guess that's why we broke it off," I realized

"I tried to hold back those feelings—"Mark started to explain

But I wasn't really listening. "Okay, Chris, what's your fucking excuse? Now I know why, every time we made love, you would have my ass up in the air. I just thought you liked doing it doggy style. Oh. I really didn't enjoy the fucking in the ass—but anything to please my man. I even went as far as to stick my finger up your ass, because you asked me to—now I know why!"

"Tina, I'm not gay, I'm bisexual. These urges come and go," said Chris

"What's the fucking difference? You want the same thing I want. A hard-ass dick under the sheets." I started pacing back and forth across the room; I couldn't help myself. I had to do something to release my pent-up energy and rage. "So, when were you going to tell me, Chris? When we got married? Or did you forget you gave me an engagement ring? And how the *fuck* did you meet Mark?"

"Over the internet," Chris said simply

"Your ass be on the fucking internet checking niggas out? So you probably checking your boys out when you be at the gym taking showers?"

"Tina, don't even go there," Chris warned.

"My homeboys are like brothers to me."

"Do any of your so-called homeboys know this shit?" I wanted to know

"Hell, naw—and I plan on keeping it that way."

I was amazed. "How the hell do you expect to keep some shit like this a fucking secret?"

"I have so far," said Chris

"Chris, *I* know now. *And* you think your boys won't find out? This shit is serious, and you fucking playing around with it. Somebody is going to fuck you up if they find out."

"I think I better go," said Mark

"No. You can stay. *I'm* leaving." I turned and started down the stairs

"Tina, wait; we need to talk!" Chris called after me

"About what, Chris? You've said it all. Once I walked my ass through the door and saw your dick pumped up in a nigga's ass, what else is there to say?"

"I need a fucking drink," said Chris

"No, *I'm* the one who need a fucking strong-ass drink," I corrected

I left them there and left the house, hoping the night air would clear my head and help me to think better. It didn't. A million thoughts kept rolling around in my brain.

Damn my ex and my fiancée, fucking each other! This is some crazy ass shit you see in the movies! I wondered if I should say something to Tracy about this. *I have to tell somebody. This shit gone eat me up.*

Well, so much for my surprise; it looks like I was the one who got the fucking surprise of the year. I have to ask myself, "Why the fuck is this happening to me? Did I do something to deserve this?" The last two men I've dealt with are fucking gay—what is going on in the world today? I need to start taking applications on a nigga. What is your sexual preference and shit? This is scary as hell; you think you're sleeping with a straight-up nigga, and he turns out to be fucking gay, or, as they say, a "switch hitter," down-low brother. I don't believe in that shit—either you prefer women or you don't. To me there's no such thing as being bisexual. Shit, in my book, if you fucking another nigga, you're gay.

But to set the record straight, I have nothing against homosexuality—"To each his own" is my motto. I have gay friends myself, so it doesn't bother me. But, when I find out that my man and my ex— Now, that's a different story. I just wish they had been up front about their sexual preference. Damn, I was definitely stuck in the dark on this one.

CHAPTER 5

"Tracy, pick up the goddamn phone!" I said

Shit! I know her ass—probably screening her fucking calls as usual. Probably dodging the damn bill collectors. I should have used my cell phone, instead of trying to sneak my ass from my office and use the copy-room phone to make a call.

"Hello, Tina, is that you?" asked Tracy, all innocence

"Your ass know you be screening your calls—caller ID is your best friend," I told her

"What's up, girl?" she asked

"I need to talk to you, and not over the phone."

"What's so fucking important you can't tell me now?"

"Just meet me at our usual spot. What I have to say I have to tell you in person."

"Ooohhhh, you pregnant!"

"Hell, naw! Pregnant is the last fucking thing I'm trying to be. Don't be fucking jinxing me," I said

"Well, you *are* engaged. Getting pregnant wouldn't be a bad thing."

"Trust me—after what I tell you, you won't be saying that shit," I said

"Damn, this must be some serious shit. Can we meet now? Your ass got me curious."

"I'll see you at six o'clock."

I hung up and looked at my watch. I better get these depositions down to the courts before they close. Derrick will be mad as hell if they aren't processed in time. I know I shouldn't be reading them, but who will know?

I sat at my desk and opened up one of the case files. Damn, this broad is crazy as hell; she must be one of them "ride or die" bitches. The transcript says that she confessed to carrying 10 kilos of coke, and that her man didn't know anything about it. Shit, I wouldn't go to jail for no nigga, fuck that!

Her ass is fucking lying. I wonder who her man is—shit, I hear somebody coming. Damn, my nosey ass got all interested in this case; now I want to know who the fuck this nigga is that this girl is going to take the rap for. Personally, I think her ass is scared as hell. Shit—it's almost five o'clock, I better get my ass over to the court. I guess I'll just punch out for the day, since I have to meet Tracy at six.

* * * * *

Screeecchh! The black Dodge Charger slammed to a halt in front of me, blocking my way. Before I could say *"What the f—"* the passenger-side window rolled down, and a masked man stuck a gun right in my face.

"Bitch, get in the fucking car!"

"Oh, my God, what the fuck is going on?" I cried, panicking

"Shut the fuck up, and get *in!*" he said

"I don't have any money, if that's what you want"

"I don't want your fucking money! I want the *envelope!*"

Then I understood. *This nigga don't want these papers to get processed. If they're turned in late, it will prolong the trial or even get the case thrown out of court.*

I'm from the streets, and I know when to shut the fuck up and save my black ass. Before I knew it, I was hauling ass, running down the street in the opposite direction. For all of you who don't know, my ass cannot run fast.

This nigga did a 180 and sped after me, dodging cars and shit.

Bump! Shit, this motherfucka hit me! I started screaming at the top of my lungs—I didn't know what the fuck to do.

Some thuggish-looking nigga ran up to me and asked, "What's the matter? What's wrong?"

"The guy in that black Dodge Charger— he's trying to kidnap me!" Before I could say anything else, this nigga punched me dead in my face and knocked me the fuck out.

*   *   *   *   *

When I woke up—vision blurred and head pounding like hell—I couldn't tell where I was, but I knew this shit was serious. A tall black man dressed in a tailor-made suit that fit his body like a glove came up to me and asked if I was okay. His voice sounded very familiar. I couldn't make out the face yet, because I still couldn't see straight. When I finally got myself together, I couldn't believe who the fuck was standing in front of me.

CHAPTER 6

"Damn, you can't even get a fucking parking spot. This shit is on jam every time I ride by here. Ain't no way in hell I'm going to waste my hard-earned money on some bitch sliding up and down a pole and grinding her pussy all up in my face," said Jason

"Whatever, nigga. You used to spend your money on them hoes," smiled Mike

"I'm a changed man," Jason told him

"Nigga, you tripping. So you a changed man in 90 days? Yeah, right—I already know, as soon as we get in there, if some good-looking broad come up in your face smiling and shit, your ass gone reach right in them pockets," laughed Mike

"Ok, bet," said Jason, reaching in his pockets right then

*   *   *   *   *

"Damn, this doesn't make any mother-fucking sense for niggas to be packed in this place like this. Damn, I'd rather have my woman give me a private dance at home. I can spend my money on her and not feel stupid as hell afterwards. At least I know who the fuck I'm giving my money to," said Mike.

The music was blasting; niggas was bumping into each other trying to get to the front of the stage. The D.J announced the next dancer.

"Men, coming to the stage for your pleasure is Jasmine. Don't touch yet, men. Let little momma get her groove on for you!"

Mike watched Jason's reaction. It was as he suspected. "No—I can't believe this shit, man! That's my woman on the stage, half naked, shaking her titties and ass like she been doing this shit forever! She climbed up the pole like a fucking pro! I think she likes doing this shit!

Monica was smiling, flicking her tongue out. She stuck her finger in her mouth and rubbed it down in between her legs. Maybe it was the 90 days in lock-up, but she got Jason's dick rising like a motherfucker. He was mad as hell, of course, but his dick was saying something else.

"You don't want to get your ass locked back up, little bro," Mike cautioned Jason, "so I let her finish her routine and followed her back stage after."

* * * * *

Jason got back stage in time to see Monica go into a dressing room. He knocked on the door.

"Who is it?" asked Monica.

"Your man," said Jason

"My man is locked up, so you must have the wrong person," said Monica

"Open the damn door, Monica!" Jason was getting impatient

"Jason, is that you?"

Monica was scared. She knew how Jason could lose his fucking mind over little shit. Her working at the strip club maybe qualified as big shit. *I hope his ass didn't see me dancing*

"I'm going to open the door, Jason—but don't come in here acting fucking crazy."

As soon as Monica opened the door, Jason snatched her up and tore her panties off. He started licking and sucking on her titties, pressing himself up against her. Monica felt his manhood rising between her legs, and she got wet immediately. Her pussy was pulsating, wanting the dick so bad she didn't know what to do. She dropped to her knees and pulled his dick out and started stroking the shaft and sucking the tip.

Monica knew what Jason liked. She knew what would relax her man; she wanted to take his mind off her dancing. Jason loved the way Monica would suck him until he was drained and couldn't move. She knew how to put a nigga out. Right now Jason was only concentrating on Monica's head movements on his dick.

"Right there, baby; yeah!" moaned Jason.

"You know how to please big daddy.
You want my dick in your pussy, don't you?"

"Fuck me, fuck me now, Jason!" screamed Monica

Jason lifted Monica up in the air and plunged his manhood into her pulsating pussy. She was hot and wet; Jason couldn't hold back—it had been three months since he'd had his dick in some pussy.

"Turn around; I want to fuck you in your ass."

"Hell, naw! That shit hurt, and it don't feel fucking good. My ass wasn't made for putting your dick into it!" Monica protested

But Jason was too strong; he turned her around and thrust his dick into her ass so hard that she started screaming. The music outside was so loud no one could hear her screams.

"Quit hollering, bitch! You know you like it."

When he saw the blood, he instantly pulled out.

"Baby, I'm sorry; I couldn't help myself," Jason apologized

"Jason, you are fucking crazy. Do you know you basically raped me?" yelled Monica, tears rolling down her cheeks.

"Baby I'm sorry. I'm so sorry," said Jason as he held her tightly to his chest.

"I know it's been three months, but—damn, baby!—you need to chill the fuck out!" cried Monica

She kept crying, because she didn't want him to start in on why she was dancing. Jason used to always tell Monica she had a dancer's body and that, if it ever got really tight for her, she could probably dance to make ends meet.
"Monica, baby, what the fuck are you doing dancing?" asked Jason, trying to stay calm.

"Remember what you used to always tell me?" asked Monica

"I didn't think you would actually do the shit! *Damn*, baby! You know I got your back; you couldn't hold on for three months? I left you enough money to get by for at least six months. I know what your ass did—you was at that fucking mall. You just can't stay away. You have got to start thinking logically, baby. What if I had to do a year? Your ass wouldn't be able to survive. I only did three months, and you out here shaking your ass in front of a bunch of niggas, calling yourself Jasmine. Them niggas just want to stick their dick in you!"

"I'm sorry baby; I didn't know what to do," said Monica

"Why didn't you go to my brother? He would have helped you out."

"I didn't want your brother to think he had to take care of me; he probably knew you had left me enough money to get by," said Monica

"Now you know, when niggas see you out on the street, what they're going to be saying. You go to college, Monica! You don't want anybody from your school to see you dancing!"

"You think I give a fuck what a motherfucka say about me? I'm living for Monica" Monica asserted. "Don't no motherfucka take care of me but you, baby, and you the only nigga I'm concerned about when it comes to me dancing. Another motherfucka ain't paying my bills, or putting food on my table. If I go through life worrying about what motherfuckas say about me, I will be stressed the fuck out. Life is too short to be worrying about what somebody feels about me. You understand what I'm saying, baby?"

"I feel you, baby—but don't think you getting off that fucking easy. After tonight, your ass better not come back up in this motherfucka. I don't care how fucking broke you get. Shit, flip some damn burgers," said Jason

"That shit ain't funny Jason. Me flipping some burgers—*shiitttt!*" said Monica

"Let's get the fuck out of here," Jason told her

CHAPTER 7

"Tracy, can I see you in my office for a moment?" asked Mr. Ward

"Yes, sir," said Tracy

She liked it when Mr. Ward asked to see her in his office. For a 50-year-old, Mr. Ward was sexy as hell. The usual stuff that always crossed her mind when she followed Mr. Ward, watching his 50-year-old ass move in his smartly tailored suits, crossed her mind now.

I know I'm kicking it with my boo, Rock, but, if this man asked to kiss my pussy with his dick, I wouldn't turn him down. Tina's always telling me that I'm going to get myself in trouble daydreaming

about Mr. Ward. But that's Tina. Tina would probably say he has worms, because he's fifty. Oh well, I can have my fantasy, and, if it happens to come true, who gives a fuck?

"Tracy how long have you been working for my company?" asked Mr. Ward

"Four years, sir."

"Have I ever offended you?"

"No—"

"I don't want to sound as if I'm hitting on you, but I think you're a really attractive young lady."

"Thank you, sir," Tracy beamed
What she really wanted to say was, "Can we fuck so I can get this out of my system?" Before she could go back to her daydreaming, Mr. Ward grabbed her breasts and started stroking them. It shocked the shit out of her. Tracy couldn't move. She got instantly hot. Her mind kept whispering, "This is not right; this is your boss—", but her pussy was telling her, "Get on that dick, girl!" She unzipped his pants and out fell a wrinkling-ass dick.

Ah, hell, naw! This can't be happening. What the fuck am I supposed to do with that?

All the excitement immediately left her body. She almost laughed out loud, holding his limp dick in her hand. *Tina told me I was going to get my ass in trouble. Now what the fuck am I going to do now? This is my boss of four years standing in front of me with his pants around his ankles and a wrinkled dick dangling in my face. Oh, well, what the fuck?*

She took ol' wrinkle ass in her hands and started to lick and kiss it. Lo and behold—ol' limp dick started to perk up; in fact, limp dick went from limp to hard-ass dick. She figured she'd better jump on that shit before the life went out of it.

* * * * *

Tracy found herself lying there on the floor, out of fucking breath. *Shit! Ol' dude wore the shit out of my pussy! It's sore as hell.* She just wanted to take her pussy home and soak in a tub.

Maybe I should ask his ol' ass if he takes Viagra or something. Maybe he did, for, as she was leaving his office, Mr. Ward told Tracy that they would meet every Friday at the same time, same place.

Shit! I wasn't expecting that. Shit! Now I'm fucked. Meeting up every week for a quickie was not in my plans. I just wanted to test the waters and keep stepping. Shit! Men do it all the time— leave a sister fast as hell after a quick fuck. Damn, what the fuck have I gotten myself into?

Stuck in the Dark   39

But Tracy didn't have a lot of time to reflect on Mr. Ward's wrinkled dick or this new wrinkle in her life. *Oh, shit, Tina's going to kill me—I'm running late.*

*   *   *   *   *

When she walked into Chili's, Tracy didn't see Tina sitting at their usual spot at the bar. She asked the waitress if Tina had shown up—everybody knew the two of them because they met at Chili's every week.

Waiting gave Tracy time to reflect—on Tina. *I wonder what the fuck was so important that she couldn't tell me over the phone. Shit, thirty minutes have passed, and still no sign of her.*

After an hour, Tracy started getting worried. She called Tina's office. No one had seen her since she had left at five o'clock. She tried her cell phone—it ended up going to voice mail. *Come on Tina, I'm getting worried now.*

After two hours passed, Tracy decided to go to the police station—where they gave her the usual line that she'd have to wait 24 hours before filing a missing person's report. There was a strange hardness in Tracy's stomach—something just wasn't right. It wasn't like Tina to just disappear. Tracy left the police station and headed to Chris's house.

It seemed like it took me forever to get to Chris house. Damn, he's not that far from the police station. Please be home.

"Chris, please tell me that Tina is here," said Tracy.

"She's not, Tracy. Why?" asked Chris

"She was supposed to meet me at Chili's at six o'clock, but she never showed up. Now I'm really worried. The last time we talked today, she said that she had something she wanted to talk to me about. She said she couldn't say it over the phone. Do you know what she could have possibly wanted to tell me?"

"No…"

Chris had a distant look on his face, as if he was thinking about something.

"Chris, are you and Tina okay? You didn't have an argument or anything did you?" asked Tracy

"No, I told you I don't know!" hollered Chris. "Don't you think I'm just as worried as you are?"

"You're right; I'm sorry. It's just that something doesn't feel right," said Tracy

"I'm sure she's okay—probably at the mall shopping," said Chris

"I really love the fact that you are being so calm about this, but, like I said, it don't feel right," Tracy said, looking around the apartment

"Chris, are you coming back up?" a male voice called from upstairs

"Who is that, Chris?" asked Tracy in shock

"Oh, just one of my old college buddies," said Chris. He had a worried look on his face

"College buddy, eh—upstairs in your bedroom?"

"Tracy, don't come at me assuming shit!" shouted Chris

"Assuming what, Chris? That you have a male friend upstairs in your bedroom, hollering downstairs asking are you coming back up? Now, you tell me what I should think. Oh, and, by the way, you're in your robe in the middle of the day, stating that I shouldn't assume something. Baby, you basically just told on yourself—and that's probably what Tina wanted to talk to me about. Did she catch you in the act, Chris? Huh?"

"Tracy, shut the fuck up, before I beat the shit out of you!"

"Oh, so now you gone beat the shit out of me? *Faggot!*"

Tracy just had time enough to think, *Why did I have to say that?* before Chris jumped up and slapped the shit out of her. She fell backwards against the table and cracked her head. It started bleeding. Feeling dizzy, she leaned on the table, trying to get up.

"What was that you said? Calling me a faggot! Look at you! Rock doesn't even know what kind of woman he has, with your sorry ass. Get the fuck up."

Chris got a crazy ass look in his eyes. For once in her life, Tracy was scared—scared that he had snapped. She knew, somehow, that she was not going to see tomorrow.

Bam, Bam! Chris hit her upside the head with a cast-iron skillet from the stove. Blood was running down Tracy's face. He dragged her to the top of the basement stairs and kicked her, sending her tumbling down. Everything went black.

CHAPTER 8

"Monica baby, wake up, I got a surprise for you," said Jason

"What, baby? It's six o'clock in the morning; what surprise do you have?" asked Monica rubbing her eyes

"Let's get married," said Jason excitedly

"Are you drunk or high, because we been together three years, and all you keep saying is, 'I ain't never getting married; shit, fuck that!'" Monica mimicked Jason. "That's your famous line."

"I'm trying to be fucking serious, and you up here playing fucking games," said Jason

"So, you *are* serious?" asked Monica

"Hell, yeah, I'm serious," said Jason

Monica sat up in bed. "Did you tell anyone else about this?"

"Not yet."

"So why now?—"

"It's just that life is too short. You're a good woman, and there's nothing out there in the streets," said Jason

"You're scaring me now, baby. Are you sure? Baby, you have got to stop with that illegal shit if you're really serious about this. You gone have to get a real nine-to-five job if you're really want to settle down and do the damn thang," said Monica

"I am serious, Monica. I already have everything set up. I'm going to tell Mike now," said Jason

"Baby, don't tell your brother right now, " said Monica looking worried. "Let's wait

"Monica, Mike's my only brother. He's the first person I'm going to tell."

"Okay, baby," Monica agreed

"Mike, big bro, come on down stairs!" Jason shouted. "I got some good news."

"What's so fucking important that it couldn't wait until I got up?" asked Mike, shambling down the steps.

"Me and Monica is getting married," said Jason excitedly

"Hell, naw!" hollered Mike, but in a tone that didn't mean, "You're kidding!", but that meant, "You're *crazy!*"

"Mike, what the fuck is wrong with you man?" asked Jason

"You just saw her last night up in a club shaking her ass for the world to see, and now you talking about *marrying* this bitch?"

"Don't be disrespecting my future wife, Mike," Jason hollered back at him. "Either you accept her or not. Because we're getting married, whether you like it or not!"

Mike walked away, slamming doors and cussing. "I can't let my little brother marry this slut! Ain't no way in hell—over my dead body! That bitch ain't worth it! I have got to come up with something—and fast—because, if I know my little brother, this nigga will up marry her today if he has the chance."

"I guess he's not gonna be best man, huh?" Monica said because she didn't know what else to say.

"Forget him," growled Jason. But Mike was all he could think of.

"Baby, can we go pick out some rings today?" Monica asked him, hoping to change the subject and take his mind off his brother. Jason turned his attention to his fiancée.

"Whatever you want, soon-to-be Mrs. Jason Davis. That sound good, don't it, boo?"

"Let's go to Clarkson's jewelry store first. I heard they have some bad ass diamond rings," said Monica

"I have to make one stop before we go to Clarkson's."

The phone rang. It was Mike, calling on his cell. He skipped the niceties. "So, you going through with this?" he asked Jason point blank

"Hell, yeah. Why not?"

Because the slut strips on stage in front of other men and does who knows what else, that's why not! But Mike just said, "Why don't you give it some more time?"

"Sorry, big bro; we are on our way to Clarkson's to pick out some rings. I'll holla back." And Jason hung up.

CHAPTER 9

"Lisa, have you seen my black shirt?" asked Tim

"Look in the hall closet. I put your clothes from the cleaners in there," Lisa told him.

"Thanks, baby."

"So, you're going to the bar with the boys?" asked Lisa

"Yeah, I won't be gone long."

On his way to the Back Door Bar Tim couldn't shake his usual nagging sense that he was somehow doing something wrong. *I always feel guilty for some reason when I go out*

Gwen Cannon

with the fellas. I guess because I'm the only one who's married, and, every time I'm out with them, they always have a table full of women. Then the females are asking me where my wife is. As long as I know I'm not doing shit, I shouldn't feel bad. I need a break every now and then just to chill with the fellas.

*   *   *   *   *

"What up, nigga, you ready for next week? We gone swoop that ass in Cleveland," said Mike.

"No doubt, nigga," said Tim.

"Where's Lisa?" asked Rock

"Where's Tracy? Nigga, don't be asking me where my wife is, and your woman ain't even here," said Tim.

"Aww, nigga, you need a drink," said Rock "Yeah, nigga, and you buying," smiled Tim

"Now that you mention it, I haven't heard from Tracy all day. She normally calls me on her way home." said Rock

"You know, Tina's her girl. Tracy and her probably stopped at the mall or something," said Tim

"Yeah, you're probably right," Rock agreed

"Mike, nigga, wake your ass up! What the fuck you over there day dreaming about?" asked G

"Man, I got some personal problems I have to deal with right now" said Mike. "I need to make a phone call."

"Shit, I hope it ain't that stripper you been fucking with," said G

"Naw, nigga, I'm straight—just got to get some shit in order," said Mike

"Is Chris coming?" asked Tim

"He said he was going to try and make it," G. explained.

"Damn, G, when you gone get a woman? You always by your fucking self. Man, you making me start to wonder," teased Rock.

"Don't worry about me, nigga. Concentrate on *your* woman," snapped G.

"Damn, man, calm the fuck down. I was just joking," said Rock.

"Shit! Fuck all that; let's toast to being homeboys for life," said Tim.

He raised his glass. "I have to say, we all are doing exactly what we said we wanted to do when we were in college together. Chris owns a travel agency; G, you still pursuing your singing career—by the way, don't lose your day job, nigga. Mike's become a sports broadcaster and owns his own show, since he messed up his knee playing pro football. Rock, you own a clothing store, and I don't know why, because your ass wear all the damn clothes. Jason is another story—smart as hell, but that fast money took control of him and his temper. He had a full baseball scholarship, but he let that fast money take control."

"Let change that toast to doing the damn thing. What's that slogan you are always saying, Tim?" asked Rock

"'Told y'all,'" laughed Tim

"Yeah, *told y'all*, motherfuckas, I was gone be my own boss," hollered Rock, laughing

"Nigga, your ass drunk already," Tim told him.

CHAPTER 10

"Monica, pick out whatever ring you like," said Jason

"Baby, I don't know. …They are all so pretty," smiled Monica

"I like that one," said Jason

"But you can't even see the diamond," said Monica, rolling her eyes

"See, I knew, if I picked that one, you would say something," laughed Jason

"Why you playing, Jason? I really need your help," whined Monica

"Okay, Okay baby, I like that one; its' five carats. You like that one?"

"Hell, yeah, baby!" screamed Monica, jumping up and hugging Jason

"Okay, that's the one then,"

"I can't wait to tell my family!"

"I love you, baby," Jason told her.

"I love you too." Then a mischievous smile played over Monica's lips. "But, are you marrying me because I'm about to graduate? You want a real woman with a real job? Huh, boo?"

"What you thought. Yep, that's exactly why I'm marrying you," joked Jason.

"Okay, say what you want, but you know the real reason. My cute little pussy snatched you up," whispered Monica seductively

"Damn, baby, you making my dick hard talking like that. You making me want some of that pussy now—see what you did?" smiled Jason, pointing to his crotch.

"Well, we can take care of that right now, boo," smiled Monica

"And how the hell we gone do that?" asked Jason, looking around the shop.

"Follow me," she said, taking him by the hand.

Jason followed Monica to the back of the store, where there was a ladies' room and a men's room. Monica pulled Jason into the men's room and started unzipping Jason's pant. As she pulled out his swollen dick, she knew it wouldn't take long to satisfy her man. She didn't care if anyone came in. She held onto his balls while she licked and flicked the tip of his dick with her tongue. He thought he was in heaven; he was thrusting his dick so hard in her mouth that she almost chocked. It didn't even take three minutes before he was grabbing her hair while his cum dripped from the side of her mouth.

"Damn, baby! I thought you were trying to kill me with your dick," Monica said, licking her lips.

"Baby, you definitely know how to please your man!" Jason pulled up his pants. "Now, let's go get my baby that ring she wants so badly."

And they did. Jason definitely knew how to please his woman.

"OOOhhh, look at my ring. It's beautiful! I'm never going to take it off," smiled Monica as tears started to form in her eyes

"Come on, baby, I know you ain't about to start crying," smiled Jason as he held Monica

"Jason, I never thought this day would come."

"You deserve it, baby. Now, go on; I'll meet you at the car. There's just one more thing I want to get. It's a surprise."

"OOhh, what is it? A tiffany bracelet?" But Monica wasn't even paying attention to herself as she strolled out of the mall, staring admiringly at her ring.

*   *   *   *   *

As Monica was approaching the car, a man came up from behind her.

"Give me your purse, bitch!" said the stranger

"What the fuck—?" Those were the last words to come out of Monica's mouth. He put the gun against the back of her head and pulled the trigger.

CHAPTER 11

I can't believe this shit!

Standing in front of me was Derrick, my fucking boss! Damn, how much money was they paying this nigga to sell out? I couldn't believe he was behind this shit. Mr. All-high-and-mighty, walking around the office like his shit didn't stank. Always telling people all he do is watch sports, play a little golf, and travel. Little did anybody know this motherfucka was out here doing some dirty, scandalous shit.

"Tina, why did you have to be so fucking nosy? I saw you take the envelope in your office, when I strictly told you to take it straight to the court. Then you just had to look at the depositions. You wouldn't be here if you would have just kept the fucking envelope closed. Now what am I going to do with you?" asked Derrick smiling

I couldn't believe my boss was in on this shit; I had to think of something—fast. These motherfuckas was not going to let me walk up out of here. The nigga who hit the shit out of me was standing off in the corner, watching me, listening to Derrick.

"I guess we're going to have to make sure you never talk, Tina," said Derrick

The nigga in the corner said, "I don't kill women or children."

"You'll kill what the fuck I tell you to kill," said Derrick

"Look, man, like I said, I ain't doing the broad."

"Give me the motherfucking gun! I'll do it!" shouted Derrick, starting toward the man, his hand held out.

"Nigga, step the fuck off," he warned Derrick. "I'm not going to stand here and watch you kill this lady. She didn't have shit to do with our original plan. Your ass up and called me at the last minute, talking about there's a change of plans. I don't know what-ever your greedy ass agreed to, but that's between you and Mike."

I wondered who the fuck this Mike was. I knew a guy named Mike, but he was a good friend of Chris who'd gone to the same college. Played professional football until he got in-jured. Then he invested in a sports broad-casting show, and was now one of the announcers. Chris and Mike were frat brothers. But there must be a million Mikes in the world; the name must just be a coincidence, I thought—until I heard the man standing in the corner elaborate.

"The nigga couldn't play football, anyway—trying to be a drug dealer and shit like his little brother! I'm glad the Feds finally caught up with his sorry ass, and I helped with that. The stupid broad he was with is dumb as fuck, taking the fall for this motherfucka. Little did he know that the stupid broad I'm talking about is my little sister. —Yeah, Derrick you didn't know that, did you? Your ass knew all about my little sis taking the fall, and you was going right along with the shit.

"I had heard about Mike—used to be this famous ex-football player trying to be in the drug game. See, this nigga was just greedy; he had money, but I guess it wasn't enough. Baby girl told me about him, how he's always up in Shake That Ass. I told my little sis exactly what to do. Flash some cash my sister's way, and she's all in with whatever plan you have. I told her just reel him in, put the pussy on him good, and make that nigga cry.

"We put a plan in place to catch his stupid ass and at the same time make a profit for ourself. We set him up real good. First, I met with the Feds to get a rap off of myself, which I was about to do a little time for. My little sis had got the nigga so caught up with the pussy and telling him how she love him that this nigga started telling her every goddamn thang. See, that's why them college-ass preppy niggas don't know shit about the streets. A real street nigga would never have told his woman shit about whatever dealing he was doing. Her ass would have thought I was only handling my sports show.

"The nigga told her when and who he was about to re-up from, and where he kept his stash. Too much motherfucking information! That's all I needed to know, I took that shit straight to the Feds. It was on and popping after that. I gave the Feds every fucking detail, from the location of his drug stash all the way up to the date of delivery. It hasn't even made it to the press yet, but, after today, the whole fucking world will know, because you know how. Old girl right here, to save her own life, she's going to take this tape recording of my conversation with you, Attorney Derrick Watts, and take it to the Feds.

"You see, when they busted Mike, my little sister told him that she loved him and that she would do anything for him. Sorry motherfucka asked her to take the fall, but little sis told him the only way she would was if he give her five hundred thousand dollars. Stupid-ass nigga fell for it too, with his weak ass.

"Now, here we have the dumb-ass lawyer—you, Derrick. I knew if we offered you enough money, your ass would fold. Your ass be losing too much money in them Goddamn casinos. See, I was watching your ass too. All you could see were dollar signs. Then you had the audacity to bring old girl over here in the picture, telling me to act like we was going to rob her. So I had one of my homeboys do it, but old girl was smart: her ass took off running—straight into me.

"Now Ms Lady, the ball's in your court. Do you want to live or die?"

CHAPTER 12

"Chris, is everything all right down there?" called Mark

"Yeah, I made a mistake and knocked over a chair in the kitchen," hollered Chris

"I could have sworn I heard a female voice—was that Tina?" asked Mark
"I said I knocked over a fucking chair!"

"Damn, what the fuck is wrong with you?" asked Mark. "Why are you getting so upset?"

"I'm just tired," said Chris

"Then come back to bed."

Chris must have been dead tired, because as soon as his head hit the pillow he was snoring like a hog.

The sound of bumping woke Mark out of his sleep. He thought maybe he was dreaming, but he kept hearing a bumping sound coming from somewhere inside the house. He decided to go downstairs and see if Chris had left the shutters to the window open. The bumping seemed to be coming from the basement. At first Mark was scared. *Maybe it's a burglar!* He grabbed a baseball bat from the closet, just in case. He slowly opened the door—and a woman with blood all over her face fell into his arms.

"Tina?" he asked. Then, when he looked more closely he could see that it was Tracy.
"What the hell happened to you?" And what are you doing here?" asked Mark.

"Chris tried to kill me . . . please help me . . . call the police . . ." Tracy managed before she collapsed

You could hear the police sirens a mile away before they arrived at Chris's apartment along with an emergency vehicle. But Chris slept through all the commotion.

"What happened here, sir?" a police officer asked Mark.

"I really don't know, officer. I found her like this. Please take her to the hospital; she's hurt really bad!" said Mark in a panic.

"Do you know who did this to her? Is there anyone else in the house?"

"No, sir, I found her like this," Mark mumbled, not meeting the policeman's eye.

"We'll need you to come down to the station to make a statement," said the police officer

"Okay. I have to put on some clothes, and I'll come down. What precinct should I go to?" asked Mark

"13th precinct off Gratiot."

Going up the stairs was the longest walk Mark ever experienced. All kinds of thoughts were going through his head. He couldn't bring his-self to believe that Chris would commit such an evil act of violence. *Should I wake him up and confront him, or should I let the police do their job? Either way it goes, once Tracy comes to, she will tell them exactly what happened. Chris, the person I have come to love with all my heart, wouldn't do this—he couldn't!*

"Chris, wake up; I have to go," Mark shook him

'Mmmhhh, where are you going?" asked Chris as he lay across the bed with his eyes closed

"I have to go make a police report," said Mark

As soon as Chris heard "police report," he jumped out of the bed and raced downstairs straight to the basement.

"How the fuck did she get out?" shouted Chris

"Chris, please tell me you didn't do that to Tracy!" screamed Mark

"She knew about me and you!" shouted Chris

"How do you know that for sure, Chris? I can't believe you would do something so evil—I don't even know if I know you anymore. Even if she did know, we can't keep hiding, Chris. The truth is going to come out sooner or later."

"I will take that to my grave before I let my family and friends know about us," shouted Chris. And he started to cry

"Chris, we can't stay stuck in the dark about our feelings for each other; we can't keep hiding," Mark passionately argued.

"I will not hurt my family with this curse!" screamed Chris" It's not a curse; we are what we are. For so long, I have felt these feelings. I kept blaming myself; I thought something was wrong with me. But I prayed and asked God for forgiveness, and I now I look at myself in a whole different light. People are going to have to accept me whether I'm gay or straight. I'm going to do what makes *Mark* happy. I'm not going to worry about what people think. I have found out that I cannot please everyone, and God did not put me on this earth to do that. A long as I know I'm not hurting anyone, I'm going to be me. Chris, you have to realize we can't please everyone—I know we both hurt Tina, but we have to move on. Life is what it is; people are going to be who they are. Whether we like it or not. So please take my hand and come with me; we'll go together. We'll weather this storm as one," said Mark.

Chris's body just shook with sobs of pain, the pain of letting go past hurts and relationships.

"I'm here for you Chris, no matter what. We'll get through this. I'll be by your side when you make your statement, trust me. It's going to be all right. 'And this too shall pass'— from the title of E. Lynn Harris's book. Come on, Chris, hold my hand and walk with me," said Mark as he held Chris.

CHAPTER 13

"Man, I gotta go; my baby is waiting for me in the parking lot. I'll holla at you later, dog," said Jason as he strolled out of the mall, smiling to himself.

As Jason got closer to the car, he could see what looked like a body lying next to the passenger-side door. Coming closer, he recognized the pink shirt Monica had put on this morning.

"No, no, noooo, not my baby! What motherfucka did this to my baby?" cried Jason

Monica lay face down in the parking lot in a puddle of blood. Jason gently picked her up in his arms and starting stroking her face. Tears streamed down his face, which bore a look of hatred that no one could possibly comprehend.

"Don't worry, baby, I'm going to get the nigga that did this, trust me on that. That's my promise to you," cried Jason as he laid Monica down, took her ring off, and walked away.

*   *   *   *   *

"Mike, I need to talk—*now*!" hollered Jason through the cell phone.

"What the fuck is wrong with you; why are you hollering in the phone?" asked Mike

"Listen, I don't need no shit from you— just meet me at the house."

"Okay, okay. I'll be there in thirty minutes" said Mike

Jason zoomed down the Lodge Freeway, breaking the speed limit, weaving his car in and out of traffic as if he were trying to kill himself. Cars were blowing their horns and swerving to avoid getting hit. Finally, he pulled up into the driveway of Mike's house. When Mike arrived, Jason was stomping around the living room, opening and closing his fist as if he wanted to punch someone.

"Jason, what the fuck is going on?" asked Mike

"Monica is dead!" shouted Jason, and he broke down, crying

"Oh, no, Jason—I'm so sorry. What the hell happened? Asked Mike as he held his brother

"We were at the mall. We had just purchased her engagement ring—" Jason looked up at his brother. Mike looked as if he hadn't heard a word Jason was saying. "Mike, Mike—*are you listening to me?* What the fuck is wrong with you?"

"Nothing, I got something important to take care of."

"I just told you that Monica is dead—and all you have to say is you got something important to take care of? I see you on some other shit—I gotta get the fuck up out of here. I'm about to make some phone calls. I got a feeling I know who did this. They probably killed Monica to get back at me." As Jason rummaged through his closet, looking for his gun

"Jason, don't go do some stupid shit. Think about it—Monica was kind of out there anyway, up in the strip club shaking her ass in front of niggas," said Mike

Gwen Cannon

"I can't believe you would say some shit like that to me! You know how I felt about her," said Jason

"Man, I'm sorry. I'm just worried about you," said Mike, giving his little brother another hug.

"Don't worry about me, big bro; I'm gone handle mine, believe that," said Jason

"Well, I gotta take care of some business, I'll holla back—and don't go do something stupid," Mike advised

CHAPTER 14

"How was your night out with the fellas?" asked Lisa

"You know, same ol' shit, same ol' drama, same bar, same people," said Tim, starting to undress.

"I don't understand—if it's the same ol' shit, why do you do it?" asked Lisa

"You know what, you're right," Tim agreed with her. "The shit is getting old, and I need to grow the fuck up. I'm not getting any younger; I want kids; I want to travel; there's so much I know we can accomplish together."

Gwen Cannon

"Baby, that's what I'm talking about, there's nothing wrong with you hanging out with your boys and having a drink, but the shit gets redundant. Every time I look up lately, you're going to the bar to meet G., Rock, Chris, or Mike. I don't say anything because I feel that's what you want to do, but I would like it if my husband would spend a little more time with me," said Lisa looking directly into Tim's eyes.

"Lisa, we can spend as much time as you want," said Tim

"Okay. I know your ass probably drunk; I'm going to repeat this same shit tomorrow and see if you remember," said Lisa, smiling

Bam, Bam, Bam!

"Who's knocking at the damn door this time of the night" asked Lisa

"I don't know, but, whoever it is, I'm going to cuss the motherfucka out. Shit, they didn't even try ringing the doorbell. Don't they know what time it is?" asked Tim

"Tim, you and Lisa need to come to the hospital now!" shouted G

"What the fuck is going on? Who's at the hospital?" asked Tim

"Tracy. Somebody beat the shit out of her and left her for dead!"

"Oh, my God!" said Lisa

"Let me grab some clothes; me and Lisa will meet you there. What hospital is she at? asked Tim

"St. Martin's on Nine Mile."

"How's Rock doing?" asked Tim

"Man, you know Rock; he ready to kill a motherfucka, but they said she slipped into a coma," said G.

"Does Tina know? She's like a sister to Tracy," said Lisa

"Naw. I tried calling her house and cell phone I didn't get an answer. I left a message."

"Did you try calling Chris's house?" suggested Lisa. "She's probably over there."

"I tried Chris's too, but I didn't get an answer there, either," said G

"Damn, that's some fucked-up shit!" said Tim

"You're telling me. Man, I'll see you at the hospital," said G.

CHAPTER 15

I stood there in that damp dark place, shaking like a fucking leaf. This nigga telling me the ball's in my court! *Of course, I want to live. I really don't know what possessed Derrick to do some stupid shit like this. He has the book smarts, but he definitely doesn't have street sense. Because, if he did, he wouldn't have let this shit play out like it did. Now this nigga about to get blasted. Whatever happens to him, his dumb ass deserves it.*

"Personally, I don't give a fuck what you do with Derrick. He didn't give a fuck about me," I said.

"*Damn*, man—old girl got back. She must have some street in her ass. Nigga, it looks like you either gone turn yourself in, or I guess you can kill yourself. I'll leave that up to you, D.," said the stranger, smiling

"Man, it don't have to be like this; I can give you some money—just please don't do this!" begged Derrick

"I ain't gone kill you. You gone pull the trigger yourself," said the stranger, still grinning.

"I don't know who you are, and I don't want to know. Please give me the tape I'll make sure I give it to the police," said Tina, still shaking.

He handed me the tape. I couldn't get out of there fast enough. The sunlight hurt my eyes. I didn't know how long I had been in there. Right now, I didn't care; I just wanted to get somewhere safe.
I need to find a taxi.

*　　*　　*　　*　　*

I had never been so glad to see my apartment. I definitely wasn't trying to go back over to Chris's apartment—fuck that.

I don't know what the fuck to do now, should I pack a bag and leave town? Or should I take this tape and go straight to the police. Damn, damn,

damn! Tina, think. If I leave town, there's a good chance that nigga will come looking for me. If I go to the police, I don't think he would try to do anything to me.

Shit, maybe now is a good time to use that number ol' boy I met at the airport gave me. Shit — where did I put his card? Damn, I know I kept it just in case. Oh, here it is. I'm going to give him a call tonight. I don't care if his office is closed; I'll leave a fucking message. I really don't know who to fucking trust. Shit, people I thought I knew ain't who I thought they were. Damn, I feel like I am going fucking crazy. Right now, I feel safer with someone I don't know. So I'm taking my chances with Attorney James Patton.

I know Tracy is probably tripping. I was supposed to meet her at six o'clock at Chili's. She probably has called everybody we know, in a fucking panic. I wonder if she tried calling Chris. Humph — wait until I tell her about Chris; nigga is a switch hitter. Damn, that shit still got me fucked up, thinking I'm about to marry this sexy-ass black brother. Who I thought had his head on straight, owned his own business. Oh well, I guess you never know who you may be sleeping next to. I still love Chris, but I'm not in love with Chris. The scene I walked in on will stay in my head forever. I know if I see him or Mark, I will see that scene with Chris *pounding away up Mark's ass. I better check my messages, I know I probably have a ton of them from Tracy.*

Beep—"You have eight unheard message."

The first few messages were just what I expected. Chris and Mark had called several times apologizing for what had happened. The next couple of messages were from Tracy; I expected that, too. Home girl was dogging me out, calling me a bitch and everything, saying that Chris was probably banging my ass to death.

Tracy, if you only knew—but I didn't get a chance to give her the details yet. Chris was probably banging *Mark's* ass right about now.

The last message made me drop to the floor, Tracy was in a coma at St. Martin's Hospital, and no one knew what had happened. The drama that I'd been through earlier was not in my thoughts right now; my only concern was getting to the hospital to check on Tracy. Tears were streaming down my face the whole way to St. Martin's. I kept trying to think of what could have possibly happened to Tracy from the last time I talked to her. I hope she didn't get caught up doing some stupid shit with her boss—I told her ass not to go there. *He's married and his wife looks like she will beat a bitch's ass in a minute.* I met Tracy's boss's wife at one of their Christmas parties. I told Tracy then, "Shit, his wife will beat the shit out of you if she catches you with her husband." But Tracy didn't care; she kept saying she wanted to fuck her boss. I told her to stop being so fucking curious. I hope her ass didn't get caught with her boss, because she told me that, if he ever propositioned her, she would be all over his ass. I told her, "Don't jump into some shit, you can't get out of."

CHAPTER 16

"I'm here to make a police report," said Mark

"What's the concern sir?" asked the desk sergeant.

"A young lady was picked up tonight; she had been badly beaten—"

"What was the young lady's name?"

"Tracy. I—I don't know her last name—"

"Do you know who beat up the young lady?"

Before Mark could answer, Chris spoke up.

"I did, officer," he confessed, wiping sweat from his forehead

"So, you're here of your own free will to make a statement?" asked the officer, looking at Chris in disbelief

"Yes."

"Okay. I'll have you sit with a detective to give your statement."

"Chris, don't worry; I'm going to stay by your side through this. I love you," said Mark, holding Chris's hand.

"Officer, can you call me at this number when you finish processing Mr. Stevens?" Mark asked, handing the detective his card.

"And, if they set a bond, please let me know."

"You can call the station in about two hours. We should have everything set by then," said the detective, leading Chris away.

"Thanks," said Mark

Several thoughts raced through his head. *I don't know what could have possessed Chris to beat Tracy the way he did. I hope and pray that she's okay. Maybe I can ask the officer what hospital she was taken to. I really just want to know if she's all right. I know I'm probably the last person she would want to see.*

The desk sergeant looked at him expectantly, wondering why he was still standing there. "Officer," Mark made up his mind to ask, "do you know what hospital the young lady who was picked up from 21107 Woodbridge was taken to?"

"Are you a relative?"

"No, I'm the one who found her and called it in. I just want to make sure she's okay."

"Right now, I can't give out any information pertaining to that incident."

"Sure. Thanks, anyway." Mark walked out into the street, feeling defeated.

Damn! The police ain't giving up any four-one-one. I guess I have to call all the nearby hospitals in our area to see if she was brought in. I guess that's the only way I will find out. I feel drained right now, I don't know if I'm coming or going. I wish today had never happened.

CHAPTER 17

"I'm going to kill the motherfucka who did this to Tracy!" cried Rock, holding his head in his hands

"Rock, you know we got your back," G told him.

"Yeah, we down for whatever," seconded Tim

"Please don't go out there and do some stupid shit," Lisa begged them.

"Lisa, no disrespect, but look at Tracy. Right now I don't give a fuck!" cried Rock

"Rock, please—for Tracy's sake—don't talk like this. Whoever did this to Tracy will not get away with it. You can't do something so brutal to someone and think that you're going to get away with it. Trust me, God will see Tracy through this," said Lisa

"I guess you don't realize how much you love someone until you think you're going to lose them," sobbed Rock, weeping into his hands.

Lisa understood. "Sometimes it takes something drastic to make you realize what you really have. Just the thought of losing them makes you go mad. —Rock, have you ever told Tracy you love her?"

"No, we've been together a year and a half, and I have never told her how I really felt. Every night, before she goes to sleep, she tells me she loves me. Now she will never get to hear me say those words to her," moaned Rock.

"It's never too late; she can hear you now. Tell her you love her Rock."

He felt a little self-conscious, but Rock took Lisa's advice. Stroking Tracy's hand, he whispered, "Tracy, if you can hear me, this is Rock, baby. I love you. I don't know why I never told you. I guess I was trying to be all hard and shit. I don't want to lose you, baby."

"Tim, baby, you're sitting back over there in the corner so quiet—what's wrong?" asked Lisa.

"I'm just looking at my beautiful wife, who I am also guilty of not saying I love you to. I know you know that I do, but I also know it feels good to hear it. Baby, I love you," smiled Tim.

"I know," smiled Lisa.

"Ok, enough with all this mushy talk—what we gone do about the motherfucka who did this?" asked G.

"Lisa's right, G.; we have to use common sense. I have to be here for Tracy now. She's really going to need me," said Rock

"Ok, but just remember—call a nigga, I'm there for whatever. You will always be my frat brother for life," said G., giving Rock a brotherly hug.

"The nurse said Tracy can hear us—why don't we say a prayer together?" asked Lisa.

"Yeah," agreed Rock. "I think Tracy would like that, just knowing her friends are here supporting her."

"Let's bow our heads," said Lisa, bowing hers. They all followed suit.

CHAPTER 18

Jason was a bundle of nervous energy. *I got to find out who shot and killed Monica, if it's the last thing I do. If Monica was set up, I know exactly who to check in with. This nigga has the scoop on every fucking thing that go down in Detroit.*

"What up Dave? You seen that nigga B.? I need to holla at him," said Jason

"Hey, dog," said Dave. "I'm sorry about Monica, man."

"How the fuck you know what happened to Monica?"

"My bad, man," Dave told him. "Shit, everybody know."

"Hold the fuck up," said Jason, looking at Dave as if he could kill him. "You telling me that Monica got shot less than five hours ago, and everybody know?"

"Wait nigga, don't be looking at me like that," Dave held up his hands. "I was at Shake That Ass, and nigga's was talking about it."

"Do you know who did this Dave? *I need to know!*" shouted Jason

"Man, I'm not trying to get into no family shit—"

"What the fuck you mean, 'in no family shit'? The only family I got living is my brother, Mike, and my father. My father has been in New Hope nursing home ever since he had a heart attack last year. So, if you trying to say my brother had something to do with Monica's death, you got to be out of your fucking mind!"

"Jason, you need to go talk to your brother—for real, dog. Ask him where the fuck he was at when Monica got shot," said Dave. ". . . By the way, who knew where you and Monica was going?"

Jason left Dave before he popped him one just for being right. *Damn! I did mention to Mike that we going to the mall to pick out an engagement ring. And Mike wasn't any too happy when I told him about me and Monica getting married. I need to talk to my big bro right now. Please God, give me strength. I need to know that my brother did not do this.* Jason dialed his brother's number, punching the hell out of his cell phone in the process. *This nigga better answer the phone.*

"Mike, I need you to meet me at the spot, right now," shouted Jason

"Man, slow the fuck down, what's going on?" asked Mike

"I think you already know, bro."
Click!

CHAPTER 19

I sped up into the hospital ramp and jumped out of the car with the keys still in the ignition. I ran up to the reception area and asked for Tracy Moore.

"She's in room 224—" said the nurse, are you a relative. Her finance and three friends are already in her room.

"I'm her sister!" I cried

"I'll have to check with her fiancé," said the nurse

"Nurse, if you don't take me to see my sister right now, I'm going to slap the shit out of you!" I screamed, tears running down my face.

"Ms, please calm down," said the nurse, rolling her eyes. "I'll take you back"

I didn't even notice anyone else in the room, I ran straight to Tracy. I fell on top of her, crying for God to heal my sister.

"Tracy, baby, I'm right here. This is T; I know you can hear me. You have to fight this shit, so we can beat the shit out of the motherfucka who did this to you!"
Someone gently lifted me from my knees.

"Come on, Tina baby; let's all hold hands and make a prayer circle around Tracy. We all have to be strong for her."

"All I can think of is who would do something like this to Tracy," I wept.

"We all are asking ourselves the same question," said G

"Did the police say anything? Who called it in? I just want to know who did this."

"We *all* want to know, Tina, but, for now—like Lisa said—we must be strong," said Rock.

"Rock," I said, looking at him as if for the first time, "I have never seen you like this before. You are always so calm and nonchalant."

"Tina, I didn't realize that I really love Tracy until now. I knew I cared for her, but this is love I'm feeling."

"A person can't help but fall in love with her," I told him, touched by his admission

I guess the nurse, who'd been standing there all this time, figured this was a good moment to interrupt. "Mr. William," she addressed Rock, "a gentleman called asking about your fiancée, Ms. Moore."

"Did he leave his name?" asked Rock

"No. I'll transfer the call to you if he calls back," said the nurse

"Thanks." Rock turned to the rest of us. "Now who would be calling to check on Tracy? We're all here, except Chris. I wonder who it is."

Looking at Tracy in this state was unbelievable. She was always the life of the party. To see her so lifeless and helpless made me want to kill the person who did this. The more I looked at Tracy, the angrier I got. I wanted to kill the motherfucka. How could someone do this to another person and leave them to die? *I need to know who found her, and—whoever that person is—find out if they saw anything. I need to talk to the police.*

CHAPTER 20

"Jason, what the fuck you talking about?" asked Mike

"Bro, you know exactly what I'm talking about. I'm only going to ask you one time, and one time only. Did you kill Monica?" asked Jason as tears started to form in his eyes

Mike looked at his brother long and hard.

"Yes," he answered.

Before Mike could react, Jason punched him in the mouth. Mike grabbed Jason by his collar and pinned him up against the wall.

"Man, why the fuck are you tripping? You saw with your own eyes what the fuck she was

doing while you were on lock down!" shouted
Mike

"Mike, I love you, but I will kill your
motherfucking ass right now. You killed the
woman I loved—who I was going to marry.
That wasn't your fucking choice to make. You
didn't have to *kill* her, Mike!"

"Okay, Jason, I see I'm going to have to
give it to you straight. Me and Monica was
fucking!" shouted Mike
Jason reached into his coat pocket, drew his
gun, and pointed it at Mike.

"So you fucked my woman, Mike?"

"Yeah, I fucked your so-called woman. She
was a slut. I couldn't stand by and watch you
throw your life away on some bitch-ass slut.
Bad enough you caught all up in the drug
game—then you want to fuck it up some more
by marrying her. Yeah, I shot her ass—and I
don't regret the shit!" screamed Mike.

"You made the statement about drugs,
nigga. I'm the one who put your sorry ass in
the drug game, and you still ain't learned shit
about that. Getting pussy-whipped and shit by
a stripper you don't know shit about. You have
the nerve to try and talk about Monica. Nigga,
please!" shouted Jason

"Jason, put the fucking gun down."

The brothers started tussling over the gun—*bam, bam!*

"Oh, shit, man—I'm sorry! Goddamn, I'm sorry! You're my brother—you can't die on me! Stay with me man; stay with me! I gotta call 911—please don't fucking die on me!"

CHAPTER 21

Mark had located what hospital Tracy had been taken to. "I hope she's okay," he muttered, running down the corridor. *Damn, I still don't understand what the fuck Chris was thinking about!*

"I'm here to see Tracy Moore, please," he told the nurse.

"Are you a relative?"

"No, I'm the one who called emergency and the police."

"Please wait here a moment," said the nurse

Mark started to pace the waiting area. Then he saw Rock coming his way. *Aw, damn! What the fuck is this nigga going to think? I'm just going to be honest and tell him straight up what happened.*

"Mark, what are you doing here?" asked Rock, genuinely surprised to see him.

"I came to check on Tracy. How's she doing."

"She's in a coma," said Rock, still wondering why Mark was there

"I need to talk to you, Rock, and please don't interrupt me. I need to get everything out in the open," said Mark

"Man, what the fuck are you talking about?"

"Listen, I found Tracy and called the police," said Mark

"What do you mean you found Tracy? And where did you find her?" asked Rock. Mark could see the anger building up in him

"Chris had beat her up and locked her in his basement," said Mark, as tears started to swell up in his eyes

"What the fuck did you say?" screamed Rock

"Tracy had come over to the house—I still don't know why she was there, but I assume her and Chris got into a confrontation about Tina," said Mark

"Man, you're losing me, what are you really saying? You mean my homeboy beat my woman into a coma—is that what you are telling me?"

"Chris is at the police station now, making a report."

"You know what? That's the best place for him, because, if I ever see him, I'm going to fucking kill him!"

"I'm really sorry about all this—I wish it never happened. I just came to see if she's okay," said Mark.

"I appreciate you calling the police, but how did you get involved in all this?" asked Rock.

"I know Chris probably will hate me for this, but—we're . . . seeing each other," said Mark, glancing sideways to see Rock's reaction.

"What do you mean 'seeing each other'? Like a *couple*?"

"Yes."

Rock looked shock.

"But—you and Chris don't look gay. I' knew Chris all through college—no way, man!"

"Gay people don't look a certain way, Rock, gay people look just like you and me."

"Chris is . . . *gay*?" asked Rock, looking uncertain.

"Yes. He was afraid that his friends wouldn't understand or accept him."

"You know, I don't understand—" said Rock.

"I don't know if you remember, but I met you once. I used to date Tina." Said Mark

"That's where I remember you from. I kept asking myself, where did I know you from? Damn—that's some fucked-up shit; I feel sorry for Tina. Her man, and her ex-man fucking. Now, that's fucked up. You know what, normally I would have run out of here looking for Chris. But I need to be here for Tracy right now. I guess it's best that he turned himself in, because I know for a fact I would have probably tried to kill him. There's no telling what could have happened."

Rock was still hung up on the gay thing.

"Damn, what's fucking me up is that we took showers in front of Chris. Shit, we were roommates all through college. Not having a fucking clue this nigga was a switch hitter. I can't blame you for what happened, but I'm just glad you found her and did what was right by calling the police. Because it could have

Gwen Cannon

turned out different. Come on, Mark; you can come see Tracy. She's still in a coma, but I'm sure she can hear you" said Rock.

CHAPTER 22

"Please don't let my brother die!" screamed Mike.

"Sir, what happened" asked the EMS attendant.

"We were playing with the gun, and it just went off. Please just hurry and get him to the hospital!"

"We're taking him to St. Martins," said the EMS attendant.

"I don't care what hospital—just please hurry!" cried Mike, as he held onto Jason's hand

*   *   *   *   *

That's was the longest ride to the hospital, I thought we would never get here.

"Sir, you can't go back into the operating room," the nurse told Mike

So he stayed outside and waited. Waited and thought. Thought and waited.

What the fuck have I done? My brother's laid up in the operating room with a bullet in his stomach and one in his arm. I know I don't pray like I should, but, God, if you're listening, please save my brother; you can you take me. I made a promise to my mother on her dying bed that I would take care of him. I don't know what is happening to me. I'm caught up in some drug charges, but that should be taken care of—baby girl is taking the rap for that. My only concern is—if and when my brother comes too, will he turn me in for Monica's murder? I can't think about that right now, I just need to make sure my brother's all right. . . . Damn! It's been two hours—I wonder what's going on.

The operating-room surgeon came out of the emergency one. Mike jumped up, expectation and panic written all over his face.

"Sir, your brother is going to be all right. We removed both bullets. However, he will have a long recovery. He was lucky neither bullet hit any of his arteries."

"Thank you, sir—that's the best news I have heard all day," said Mike

"Mike—is that *you*?" asked Rock as he was walking down the hospital corridor

"What are you doing here?" asked Mike, wondering if Rock knew what had happened

"Tracy is in a coma—that nigga Chris beat her up."

"Man, you have got to be lying! What the fuck was that nigga on?" asked Mike in shock

"Man, how much time do you have, because you are going to have to take a seat to hear this shit. Matter of fact, maybe you should come down to Tracy's room. Tim, Lisa, Tina, G., and Chris's friend Mark are here. . . .There's something about Chris we all didn't know."

CHAPTER 23

"Hello, may I speak to Attorney James Patton?" I asked

"Attorney Patton speaking. How may I help you?"

"This is Tina Baker. We met a few weeks ago at the airport. You flagged down a cab for me and gave me your card."

"Oh, I remember—the beautiful sister with the trench coat on."

"I think I need your services."

"We can meet tomorrow at eight a.m. at Starbucks on Jefferson," he suggested.

"That's sounds good; I'll see you tomorrow."

I feel better already, after talking to Mr.
Patton. I need to go back in the room and check
on Tracy.

"I think she's waking up," said Lisa

"Oh, my God, she's opening her eyes!" I
pointed

Rock ran over to the bed and just started
kissing Tracy all over her face and telling her
how much he loved her.

Tracy looked around the room, just then
realizing that all her friends were there. She
was especially shocked to see Mark—she just
looked at him and started crying. She suddenly
reached out for him. Mark came over to the
bed, and Tracy grabbed his hand. It seemed
like she wanted to tell him something, but she
couldn't talk. But she didn't have to say
anything. Mark seemed to know just by her
expression what she was trying to telling him.

"Tracy, you don't have to thank me.
Anyone would have done the same thing,"
said Mark

"What going on?" asked Tina

"Mark's the one who saved Tracy." Rock
turned to Mark. "Do you want to tell everyone
what happened or shall I?"

Mark told. He told them about everything that happened with Tracy and Chris. I couldn't believe what I was hearing. Chris didn't seem like the type to beat a woman. Tim and Lisa were shocked to find out that Chris and Mark were sleeping together.

After Mark finished his story, we all just sat there, staring at each other. I was the first to say something.

"Is there anything we should know about each other that we thought we knew?"

Everyone was silent, wondering if anyone else would speak first, wondering if they should say anything. Then Mike blurted out, "I shot my brother today, and he's here at St. Martin's. I sell drugs, and I might be going to jail if it don't work out like my lawyer planned."

"Mike, I know all about your drug dealing," I told him.

"What do you mean, Tina?"

"I was kidnapped earlier today. My boss, Derrick, set me up."

"All this time, I didn't know you worked for Derrick," said Mike

"The nigga that kidnapped me set you up, Mike. So be prepared to go to jail. He had his sister in on it."

"Who is his sister?" asked Mike

"The dancer you were seeing from Shake That Ass." Everyone looked around in shock

"How did *you* get involved in this, Tina?" asked Mike

"My nosy ass read your file, not knowing at the time it was you."

"Damn, my life is fucked up. I can't say anything else. You will probably hear about it on the news," said Mike. He left the room
We were all sitting there, wondering what else could go wrong. "I guess we'll have to watch the news," said Tina, looking over at her best friend

There was silence in the room as the news broadcast came on.

Gwen Cannon

CHAPTER 24

"It looks like everything is in order," said Attorney Patton

"I just want this to be over; this has been the longest two months." I told him

"I hate you had to go through all this," said Attorney Patton

"I just hate the fact that my friends and people I thought I knew were involved."

"Yeah. Life brings unexpected things in your path; it's up to you to make the right choices in life."

"I'm so glad my girl Tracy is doing okay. She's going to get married next month. I hope she know who she's marrying. The bomb I got dropped on me is still unbelievable. Are there any secrets you want to tell me about yourself before we go out on this date later?"

"Hell, naw. I'm straight up, Ms. Baker. I like a soft sensuous body next to me; I don't want to wake up next to a hard-ass body; that's not me."

"I really feel bad about Mike. I thought he was one of the few good brothers we have out here today."

"I think he just got caught up, trying to be something he wasn't. Now, your ex-boss is going to prison for 25 years and losing his license to practice. That's fucked up—to put all your efforts into something you love and get lost for the love of money," said Attorney Patton

"I think I'm going to go to Chris and Mike's trials. Chris trial starts today in ten minutes. I want to ask him why he did what he did to Tracy. But I guess it's better left unsaid. Rock seems to be handling it well; he's always so calm and cool. I'm still tripping about how Mike just killed his brother's girlfriend."

"Mike really got into some deep shit—drugs and murder. He's lucky his brother

Gwen Cannon

didn't press charges, too." said Attorney Patton

"I know. I hope everything works out for them. Jason is in physical therapy, and he seems to being coming along."

"You ready, Miss Lady?" asked Attorney Patton

"Yeah, I want to get in the court room before they stop letting anyone in."
Bam, Bam, Bam!

"Shit—what the fuck was *that*?" asked Attorney Patton, pulling Tina down on the floor.

"It sounded like it came from the hallway—how the fuck did someone get in the court house with a gun?"

"Let's get out of here!" said Attorney Patton.

We started carefully walking down the courthouse corridor, but then—"Oh, my God! It can't be!" I shouted in shock.

I ran toward the body laid out on the courthouse floor. I couldn't believe my eyes. Chris lay in a puddle of blood; people were running through the courthouse screaming and bumping into each other trying to get out.

No one paid attention to Rock standing in the back of the crowd with a look of pleasure. He showed no remorse over what he had just done.

About the Author

Gwen Cannon, a native of Detroit, Michigan, currently resides in Dearborn, Michigan. She was educated in the Detroit Public School System. She earned a Bachelor's degree in Business Management from Cornerstone University and an MBA in Business Administration.

Gwen is employed as a Release Analyst with Renaissance Global Logistics. In her spare time, she loves to read, cook, write poetry, and play Co-ed softball and her new forte in life an up and coming author. She was so intrigued with reading various novels that it inspired her to write one herself. *Stuck in the Dark* is her second novel and a work of fiction. She is happily married to her soul mate James Cannon, and they have five sons, James Jr., Corey, Jonathan, Jordan, and Jalen, and one granddaughter, Co'Mya.

COMING SOON

"Scandalous"

For additional information, contact:

Gwen Cannon
P.O. Box 44-740
Detroit, MI 48244
ph: 313-982-2093
info@gwencannon.net

Website: www.gwencannon.net